ST. THERESA SCHOOL
300 Leonard Street
Hellertown, Pa. 18055

ST. THERESA SCHOOL
300 Leonard Street
Hellertown, Pa. 18055

f.
A i c

RAINBOW CLASSICS

General Editor: May Lamberton Becker

Jo's Boys

A SEQUEL TO *LITTLE MEN*

LOUISA MAY ALCOTT

Illustrated by GRACE PAULL

Introduction by MAY LAMBERTON BECKER

THE WORLD PUBLISHING COMPANY

Cleveland and New York

Rainbow Classics

are published by THE WORLD PUBLISHING COMPANY

2231 WEST 110TH STREET, CLEVELAND 2, OHIO

PUBLISHED SIMULTANEOUSLY IN CANADA BY

NELSON, FOSTER & SCOTT LTD.

Library of Congress Catalog Card Number: 57-7409

3CP566

To

DR. CONRAD WESSELHOEFT

This very inadequate tribute

of affection and respect

is gratefully inscribed

by his friend and patient,

The Author

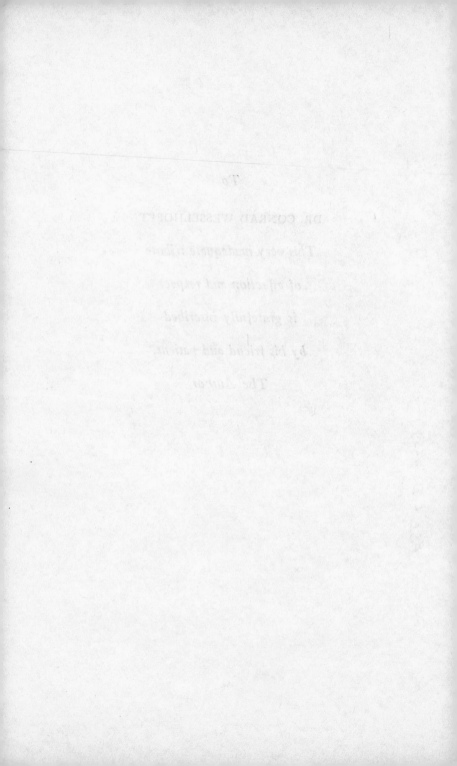

Contents

Introduction

HOW THIS BOOK CAME TO BE WRITTEN

by May Lamberton Becker

LOUISA MAY ALCOTT spent more time on *Jo's Boys* than on any other chronicle of the March family; it was in her mind or on her desk for four years. It was scarcely under way—in a hotel room to which she had retreated to work without interruptions—when her father, gentle, scholarly Bronson Alcott, had a paralytic stroke that left him helpless. Louisa and Anna sprang to his help, as Joe and Meg would have done, and nursed him as long as he needed their care. Emerson, the Alcotts' never-failing family friend, had left the world not long before, as gently as "Marmee" had gone, though not at so advanced an age. May, who had met and married a Swiss gentleman while studying abroad, had died in 1879, a month after her baby, Louisa's namesake, was born. The inner circle of the March family, the Alcotts of Orchard House, Concord, was narrowing. Louisa adopted Anna's son John Pratt to take the name of Alcott and attend to her royalties as her literary executor; they would still be taking care of the family when she had ended her long labor of love. May's baby, blue-eyed Louisa May Nieriker, had arrived; May had asked, before her baby was born, that if she herself should not live, Lulu should go to Louisa in America. Aunt Louisa, who had hoped and longed to take all the care of her precious legacy,

7

found her own health not so robust as that of the bouncing baby, and instead created for Lulu a nursery with trained attendance, filled with everything by which she could express her love for the lost sister and her devotion to the motherless child.

All this took careful supervision, and Louisa's fame took much of her time besides. She did as much as she could to escape the attention of a world-wide public, but it could not be altogether kept from breaking in, as she tells us with such fun in the second chapter of this book. For the Ugly Duckling of the Alcotts had long since turned out to be, in her own words, "not a swan, but a golden goose, whose literary eggs found such an unexpected market that in ten years Jo's wildest and most cherished dream actually came true." Now she was worn and tired; instead of the furious scribbling, the joyous rush of her earlier work, she now could sometimes write no more than two hours a day. Her pen grew heavy; she often had to lay it down for weeks at a time. But she always picked it up again and went on writing until *Jo's Boys* was finished at Concord in 1886.

What kept her writing on this book so long, and for all her interruptions, so steadily? She must have known it was not one of her best. She no longer had to write for money; her "most cherished dream" of providing for the family had come true. Far in the past were the days when the Alcott girls had to wear, however gaily, the made-over clothes of their rich relations, paint their shoes, and if one glove was past wearing, bravely carry the other in the hand. Never ashamed of poverty, Louisa was proud that she could take her beloved family out of it. No one sent back her manuscripts now; thousands of children all over the English-speaking world were crying out in letters to her publishers and to her for more and yet more stories.

It was indeed for them that Louisa was now writing. She

knew that they couldn't bear to leave the charmed circle of the March family on the last page of *Little Men*. They wanted to know "what became of" not only the twelve original boys of Plumfield, Franz and Emil, Nat the musician, Dan the wanderer and all the rest, but the little people who had come into the story as it went on, such as Bess and Josie and the irrepressible Teddy. Louisa Alcott understood children so well that she felt as they did about this, and meant to satisfy them. Besides, she understood her dream children so well she could foresee what they would do, even unto the third generation. Now she would round them up and tell what became of everyone. She knew she would not write much longer—that heavy pen told her so. But before she laid it down, she would have met those dream children once more and found out what happened to them in their later lives.

So there is not in *Jo's Boys* that close tie with actual life in the Alcott family that gave *Little Women* its immediate and lasting charm and swept *Little Men* along with it into children's hearts. There was no Plumfield in real life, and Laurence College is only indirectly related to the Concord School of Philosophy, that noble undertaking that came just in time to bring Bronson Alcott a belated recognition. With many marriages and as few deaths as possible, everyone in the widened circle of Mrs. Josephine Bhaer's friends and family was accounted for. From now on, Louisa wrote only a few short stories such as Lulu might read. The curtain had fallen forever on the March family.

Preface

HAVING been written at long intervals during the past seven years, this story is more faulty than any of its very imperfect predecessors; but the desire to atone for an unavoidable disappointment, and to please my patient little friends, has urged me to let it go without further delay.

To account for the seeming neglect of AMY, let me add that, since the original of that character died, it has been impossible for me to write of her as when she was here to suggest, criticize, and laugh over her namesake. The same excuse applies to MARMEE. But the folded leaves are not blank to those who knew and loved them, and can find memorials of them in whatever is cheerful, true, or helpful in these pages.

L. M. ALCOTT

Concord, July 4, 1886

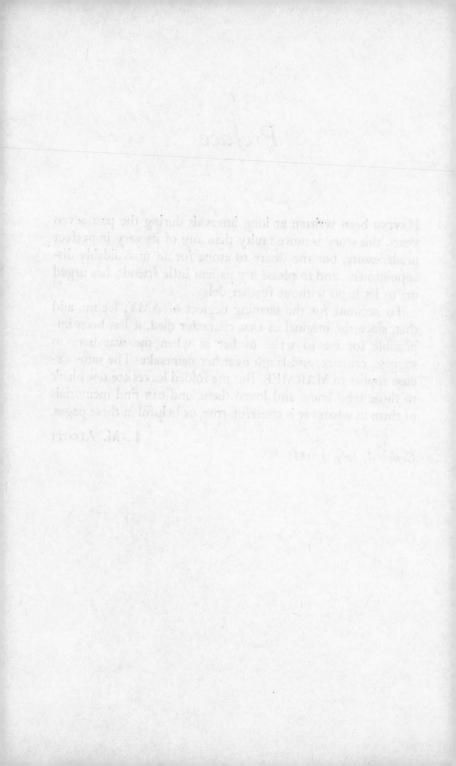

Jo's Boys

1. Ten Years Later

"I F ANYONE had told me what wonderful changes were to take place here in ten years, I wouldn't have believed it," said Mrs. Jo to Mrs. Meg, as they sat on the piazza at Plumfield one summer day, looking about them with faces full of pride and pleasure.

"This is the sort of magic that money and kind hearts can work. I am sure Mr. Laurence could have no nobler monument than the college he so generously endowed; and a home like this will keep Aunt March's memory green as long as it lasts," answered Mrs. Meg, always glad to praise the absent.

"We used to believe in fairies, you remember, and plan what we'd ask for if we could have three wishes. Doesn't it seem as if mine had been really granted at last? Money, fame, and plenty of the work I love," said Mrs. Jo, carelessly rumpling up her hair as she clasped her hands over her head just as she used to do when a girl.

"I have had mine, and Amy is enjoying hers to her heart's content. If dear Marmee, John, and Beth were here, it would be quite perfect," added Meg, with a tender quiver in her voice; for Marmee's place was empty now.

Jo put her hand on her sister's, and both sat silent for a little while, surveying the pleasant scene before them with mingled sad and happy thoughts.

It certainly did look as if magic had been at work, for quiet Plumfield was transformed into a busy little world. The house seemed more hospitable than ever, refreshed with new paint, added wings, well-kept lawn and garden, and a prosperous air it had not worn when riotous boys swarmed everywhere and it was rather difficult for the Bhaers to make both ends meet. On the hill, where kites used to be flown, stood the fine college which Mr. Laurence's munificent legacy had built. Busy students were going to and fro along the paths once trodden by childish feet, and many young men and women were enjoying all the advantages that wealth, wisdom, and benevolence could give them.

Just inside the gates of Plumfield a pretty brown cottage, very like the Dovecote, nestled among the trees, and on the green slope westward Laurie's white-pillared mansion glittered in the sunshine; for when the rapid growth of the city shut in the old house, spoilt Meg's nest, and dared to put a soap factory under Mr. Laurence's indignant nose, our friends emigrated to Plumfield, and the great changes began.

These were the pleasant ones; and the loss of the dear old people was sweetened by the blessings they left behind; so all prospered now in the little community, and Mr. Bhaer as president, and Mr. March as chaplain, of the college, saw their long-cherished dream beautifully realized. The sisters divided the care of the young people among them, each taking the part that suited her best. Meg was the motherly friend of the young women, Jo the confidante and defender of all the youths, and Amy the Lady Bountiful who delicately smoothed the way for needy students, and entertained them all so cordially that it was no wonder they named her lovely home Mount Parnassus, so full was it of music, beauty, and the culture hungry young hearts and fancies long for.

The original twelve boys had of course scattered far and wide during these years, but all that lived still remembered old Plumfield, and came wandering back from the four quarters of the earth to tell their various experiences, laugh over the pleasures of the past, and face the duties of the present with fresh courage; for such home-comings keep hearts tender and hands helpful with the memories of young and happy days. A few words will tell the history of each, and then we can go on with the new chapter of their lives.

Franz was with a merchant kinsman in Hamburg, a man of twenty-six now, and doing well. Emil was the jolliest tar that ever "sailed the ocean blue." His uncle sent him on a long voyage to disgust him with this adventurous life; but he came home so delighted with it that it was plain this was his profession, and the German kinsman gave him a good chance in his ships; so the lad was happy. Dan was a wanderer still; for after the geological researches in South America he tried sheep farming in Australia, and was now in California looking up mines. Nat was busy with music at the Conservatory, preparing for a year or two in Germany to finish him off. Tom was studying medicine and trying to like it. Jack was in business with his father, bent on getting rich. Dolly was in college with Stuffy and Ned reading law. Poor little Dick was dead, so was Billy; and no one could mourn for them, since life would never be happy, afflicted as they were in mind and body.

Rob and Teddy were called the "Lion and the Lamb"; for the latter was as rampant as the king of beasts, and the former as gentle as any sheep that ever baaed. Mrs. Jo called him "my daughter," and found him the most dutiful of children, with plenty of manliness underlying the quiet manners and tender nature. But in Ted she seemed to see all the faults, whims, aspirations, and fun of her own youth in a new shape. With his tawny locks always in wild confusion, his long legs and arms, loud voice, and continual activity, Ted was a prominent figure at Plumfield. He had his moods of gloom, and fell into the Slough of Despond about once a week, to be hoisted out by patient Rob or his mother, who understood when to let him alone and when to shake him up. He was her pride and joy as well as torment, being a very bright lad for his age and so full of all sorts of budding talent that her maternal mind was much exercised as to what this remarkable boy would become.

Demi had gone through college with honor, and Mrs. Meg had set her heart on his being a minister—picturing in her fond fancy the first sermon her dignified young parson would preach, as well as the long, useful, and honored life he was to lead. But John, as she called him now, firmly declined the divinity school, saying he had had enough of books and needed to know more of men and the world, and caused the dear woman much disappointment by deciding to try a journalist's career. It was a blow; but she knew that young minds cannot be driven, and that experience is the best teacher; so she let him follow his own inclinations, still hoping to see him in the pulpit. Aunt Jo raged when she found that there was to be a reporter in the family, and called him "Jenkins" on the spot. She liked his literary tendencies, but had reason to detest official Paul Prys, as we shall see later. Demi knew his own mind, however, and tranquilly carried out his plans, unmoved by the tongues of the anxious mammas or the jokes of his mates. Uncle Teddy encouraged him, and painted a splendid career, mentioning Dickens and other celebrities who began as reporters and ended as famous novelists or newspapermen.

The girls were all flourishing. Daisy, as sweet and domestic as ever, was her mother's comfort and companion. Josie at fourteen was a most original young person, full of pranks and peculiarities, the latest of which was a passion for the stage, which caused her quiet mother and sister much anxiety as well as amusement. Bess had grown into a tall, beautiful girl, looking several years older than she was, with the same graceful ways and dainty tastes which the little Princess had, and a rich inheritance of both the father's and mother's gifts, fostered by every aid love and money could give. But the pride of the community was Naughty Nan; for, like so many restless, willful children, she was growing into a woman full of the energy and promise that suddenly blossoms when the ambitious seeker finds the work she is fitted to do well. Nan began to study medicine at sixteen, and at twenty was getting on bravely; for now, thanks to other intelligent women, colleges and hospitals were open to her. She had never wavered in her purpose from the childish days when she shocked Daisy in the old willow by saying, "I don't want any family to fuss over. I shall have an office, with bottles and pestle things in it, and drive round and cure folks." The future foretold by the little girl the young woman was rapidly bringing to pass, and finding so much happiness in it that nothing could win her from the chosen work. Several worthy young gentlemen had tried to make her change her mind and choose, as Daisy did, "a nice little house and a family to take care of." But Nan only laughed, and routed the lovers by proposing to look at the tongue which spoke of adoration, or professionally felt the pulse in the manly hand offered for her acceptance. So all departed but one persistent youth, who was such a devoted Traddles it was impossible to quench him.

This was Tom, who was as faithful to his child sweetheart as she to her "pestle things," and gave a proof of fidelity that touched her very much. He studied medicine for her sake alone, having no taste for it, and a decided fancy for a mercantile life. But Nan was firm, and Tom stoutly kept on, devoutly hoping he might not kill many of his fellow beings when he came to practice. They were excellent friends, however, and caused much amusement to their comrades by the vicissitudes of this merry love chase.

Both were approaching Plumfield on the afternoon when Mrs. Meg and Mrs. Jo were talking on the piazza. Not together; for Nan was walking briskly along the pleasant road alone, thinking over a case that interested her, and Tom was pegging on behind to overtake her, as if by accident, when the suburbs of the city were past—a little way of his, which was part of the joke.

Nan was a handsome girl, with a fresh color, clear eye, quick smile, and the self-poised look young women with a purpose always have. She was simply and sensibly dressed, walked easily, and seemed full of vigor, with her broad shoulders well back, arms swinging freely, and the elasticity of youth and health in every motion. The few people she met turned to look at her, as if it was a pleasant sight to see a hearty, happy girl walking countryward that lovely day; and the red-faced young man steaming along behind, hat off and every tight curl wagging with impatience, evidently agreed with them.

Presently a mild "Hullo!" was borne upon the breeze, and pausing, with an effort to look surprised that was an utter failure, Nan said affably:

"Oh, is that you, Tom?"

"Looks like it. Thought you might be walking out today."
Tom's jovial face beamed with pleasure.

"You knew it. How is your throat?" asked Nan in her professional tone, which was always a quencher to undue rap-
tures.

"Throat? Oh, ah! yes, I remember. It is well. The effect
of that prescription was wonderful. I'll never call homeop-
athy a humbug again."

"You were the humbug this time, and so were the unmed-
icated pellets I gave you. If sugar of milk can cure diphthe-
ria in this remarkable manner, I'll make a note of it. Oh,
Tom, Tom, will you never be done playing tricks?"

"Oh, Nan, Nan, will you never be done getting the better
of me?" And the merry pair laughed at one another just
as they did in the old times, which always came back freshly
when they went to Plumfield.

"Well, I knew I shouldn't see you for a week if I didn't
scare up some excuse for a call at the office. You are so des-
perately busy all the time I never get a word," explained
Tom.

"You ought to be busy too, and above such nonsense.
Really, Tom, if you don't give your mind to your lectures,
you'll never get on," said Nan soberly.

"I have quite enough of them as it is," answered Tom, with
an air of disgust. "A fellow must lark a bit after dissecting
corpuses all day. I can't stand it long at a time, though *some
people* seem to enjoy it immensely."

"Then why not leave it, and do what suits you better? I
always thought it a foolish thing, you know," said Nan, with
a trace of anxiety in the keen eyes that searched for signs
of illness in a face as ruddy as a Baldwin apple.

"You know why I chose it, and why I shall stick to it if it
kills me. I may not *look* delicate, but I've a deep-seated heart

complaint, and it will carry me off sooner or later; for only one doctor in the world can cure it, and she won't."

There was an air of pensive resignation about Tom that was both comic and pathetic; for he was in earnest, and kept on giving hints of this sort without the least encouragement.

Nan frowned; but she was used to it, and knew how to treat him.

"She *is* curing it in the best and only way; but a more refractory patient never lived. Did you go to that ball, as I directed?"

"I did."

"And devote yourself to pretty Miss West?"

"Danced with her the whole evening."

"No impression made on that susceptible organ of yours?"

"Not the slightest. I gaped in her face once, forgot to feed her, and gave a sigh of relief when I handed her over to her mamma."

"Repeat the dose as often as possible, and note the symptoms. I predict that you will 'cry for it' by and by."

"Never! I'm sure it doesn't suit my constitution."

"We shall see. Obey orders!" sternly.

"Yes, doctor," meekly.

Silence reigned for a moment; then, as if the bone of contention was forgotten in the pleasant recollections called up by familiar objects, Nan said, suddenly:

"What fun we used to have in that wood! Do you remember how you tumbled out of the big nut tree and nearly broke your collarbone?"

"Don't I! And how you steeped me in wormwood till I was a fine mahogany color, and Aunt Jo wailed over my spoilt jacket," laughed Tom, a boy again in a minute.

"And how you set the house afire?"

"And you ran off for your bandbox?"

"Do you ever say 'Thunder-turtles' now?"

"Do people ever call you 'Giddy-gaddy'?"

"Daisy does. Dear thing, I haven't seen her for a week."

"I saw Demi this morning, and he said she was keeping house for Mother Bhaer."

"She always does when Aunt Jo gets into a vortex. Daisy is a model housekeeper; and you couldn't do better than make your bow to her, if you can't go to work and wait till you are grown up before you begin lovering."

"Nat would break his fiddle over my head if I suggested such a thing. No, thank you. Another name is engraved upon my heart as indelibly as the blue anchor on my arm. 'Hope' is my motto, and 'No surrender,' yours; see who will hold out longest."

"You silly boys think we must pair off as we did when children; but we shall do nothing of the kind. How well Parnassus looks from here!" said Nan, abruptly changing the conversation again.

"It is a fine house; but I love old Plum best. Wouldn't Aunt March stare if she could see the changes here?" answered Tom, as they both paused at the great gate to look at the pleasant landscape before them.

A sudden whoop startled them, as a long boy with a wild yellow head came leaping over a hedge like a kangaroo, followed by a slender girl, who stuck in the hawthorn, and sat there laughing like a witch. A pretty little lass she was, with curly dark hair, bright eyes, and a very expressive face. Her hat was at her back, and her skirts a good deal the worse for the brooks she had crossed, the trees she had climbed, and the last leap, which added several fine rents.

"Take me down, Nan, please. Tom, hold Ted; he's got my book, and I *will* have it," called Josie from her perch, not at all daunted by the appearance of her friends.

Tom promptly collared the thief, while Nan picked Josie from among the thorns and set her on her feet without a

"Mrs. Bhaer never sees reporters, sir." (page 59)

word of reproof; for having been a romp in her own girl-
hood, she was very indulgent to like tastes in others. "What's
the matter, dear?" she asked, pinning up the longest rip, while
Josie examined the scratches on her hands.

"I was studying my part in the willow, and Ted came
slyly up and poked the book out of my hands with his rod.
It fell in the brook, and before I could scrabble down he
was off. You wretch, give it back this moment or I'll box
your ears," cried Josie, laughing and scolding in the same
breath.

Escaping from Tom, Ted struck a sentimental attitude, and
with tender glances at the wet, torn young person before him,
delivered Claude Melnotte's famous speech in a lackadaisical
way that was irresistibly funny, ending with "Dost like the
picture, love?" as he made an object of himself by tying his
long legs in a knot and distorting his face horribly.

The sound of applause from the piazza put a stop to these
antics, and the young folks went up the avenue together very
much in the old style when Tom drove four in hand and
Nan was the best horse in the team. Rosy, breathless, and
merry, they greeted the ladies and sat down on the steps to
rest, Aunt Meg sewing up her daughter's rags while Mrs. Jo
smoothed the Lion's mane, and rescued the book. Daisy ap-
peared in a moment to greet her friend, and all began to talk.

"Muffins for tea; better stay and eat 'em; Daisy's never
fail," said Ted hospitably.

"He's a judge; he ate nine last time. That's why he's so
fat," added Josie, with a withering glance at her cousin, who
was as thin as a lath.

"I must go and see Lucy Dove. She has a whitlow, and it's
time to lance it. I'll tea at college," answered Nan, feeling
in her pocket to be sure she had not forgotten her case of
instruments.

"Thanks, I'm going there also. Tom Merryweather has

granulated lids, and I promised to touch them up for him. Save a doctor's fee and be good practice for me. I'm clumsy with my thumbs," said Tom, bound to be near his idol while he could.

"Hush! Daisy doesn't like to hear you sawbones talk of your work. Muffins suit us better"; and Ted grinned sweetly, with a view to future favors in the eating line.

"Any news of the Commodore?" asked Tom.

"He is on his way home, and Dan hopes to come soon. I long to see my boys together, and have begged the wanderers to come to Thanksgiving, if not before," answered Mrs. Jo, beaming at the thought.

"They'll come, every man of them, if they can. Even Jack will risk losing a dollar for the sake of one of our jolly old dinners," laughed Tom.

"There's the turkey fattening for the feast. I never chase him now, but feed him well; and he's 'swellin' wisibly,' bless his drumsticks!" said Ted, pointing out the doomed fowl proudly parading in a neighboring field.

"If Nat goes the last of the month we shall want a farewell frolic for him. I suppose the dear old Chirper will come home a second Ole Bull," said Nan to her friend.

A pretty color came into Daisy's cheek, and the folds of muslin on her breast rose and fell with a quick breath; but she answered placidly, "Uncle Laurie says he has *real* talent, and after the training he will get abroad he can command a good living here, though he may never be famous."

"Young people seldom turn out as one predicts, so it is of little use to expect anything," said Mrs. Meg, with a sigh. "If our children are good and useful men and women, we should be satisfied; yet it's very natural to wish them to be brilliant and successful."

"They are like my chickens, mighty uncertain. Now, that fine-looking cockerel of mine is the stupidest one of the lot, and the ugly, long-legged chap is the king of the yard, he's so smart; crows loud enough to wake the Seven Sleepers; but the handsome one croaks, and is no end of a coward. *I* get snubbed; but you wait till I grow up, and then see." Ted looked so like his own long-legged pet that everyone laughed at his modest prediction.

"I want to see Dan settled somewhere. 'A rolling stone gathers no moss,' and at twenty-five he is still roaming about the world without a tie to hold him, except this," and Mrs. Meg nodded toward her sister.

"Dan will find his place at last, and experience is his best teacher. He is rough still, but each time he comes home I see a change for the better, and never lose my faith in him. He may never do anything great, or get rich; but if the wild boy makes an honest man, I'm satisfied," said Mrs. Jo, who always defended the black sheep of her flock.

"That's right, mother, stand by Dan! He's worth a dozen Jacks and Neds bragging about money and trying to be swells. You see if he doesn't do something to be proud of and take the wind out of their sails," added Ted, whose love for his "Danny" was now strengthened by a boy's admiration for the bold, adventurous man.

"Hope so, I'm sure. He's just the fellow to do rash things and come to glory—climbing the Matterhorn, taking a 'header' into Niagara, or finding a big nugget. That's his way of sowing wild oats and perhaps it's better than ours," said Tom thoughtfully; for he had gained a good deal of experience in that sort of agriculture since he became a medical student.

"Much better!" said Mrs. Jo emphatically. "I'd rather send my boys off to see the world in that way than leave them alone in a city full of temptations, with nothing to do but waste time, money, and health, as so many are left. Dan has to work his way, and that teaches him courage, patience, and self-reliance. I don't worry about him as much as I do about George and Dolly at college, no more fit than two babies to take care of themselves."

"How about John? He's knocking round town as a news-paperman, reporting all sorts of things, from sermons to prize fights," asked Tom, who thought that sort of life would be much more to his own taste than medical lectures and hos-pital wards.

"Demi has three safeguards—good principles, refined tastes, and a wise mother. He won't come to harm, and these ex-periences will be useful to him when he begins to write, as I'm sure he will in time," began Mrs. Jo in her prophetic tone; for she was anxious to have some of her geese turn out swans.

"Speak of Jenkins, and you'll hear the rustling of his paper," cried Tom, as a fresh-faced, brown-eyed young man came up the avenue, waving a newspaper over his head.

"Here's your *Evening Tattler!* Latest edition! Awful mur-der! Bank clerk absconded! Powder mill explosion, and great strike of the Latin School boys!" roared Ted, going to meet his cousin with the graceful gait of a young giraffe.

"The Commodore is in, and will cut his cable and run before the wind as soon as he can get off," called Demi, with "a nice derangement of nautical epitaphs," as he came up smiling over his good news.

Everyone talked together for a moment, and the paper passed from hand to hand that each eye might rest on the pleasant fact that the *Brenda*, from Hamburg, was safe in port.

"He'll come lurching out by tomorrow with his usual col-lection of marine monsters and lively yarns. I saw him, jolly and tarry and brown as a coffeeberry. Had a good run, and hopes to be second mate, as the other chap is laid up with a broken leg," added Demi.

"Wish I had the setting of it," said Nan to herself, with a professional twist of her hand.

"How's Franz?" asked Mrs. Jo.

"He's going to be married! There's news for you. The first of the flock, aunty, so say good-by to him. Her name is Ludmilla Hildegard Blumenthal; good family, well off, pretty, and of course an angel. The dear old boy wants uncle's consent, and then he will settle down to be a happy and an honest burgher. Long life to him!"

"I'm glad to hear it. I do so like to settle my boys with a good wife and a nice little home. Now, if all is right, I shall feel as if Franz was off my mind," said Mrs. Jo, folding her hands contentedly; for she often felt like a distracted hen with a large brood of mixed chickens and ducks upon her hands.

"So do I," sighed Tom, with a sly glance at Nan. "That's what a fellow needs to keep him steady; and it's the duty of nice girls to marry as soon as possible, isn't it, Demi?"

"If there are enough nice fellows to go round. The female population exceeds the male, you know, especially in New England; which accounts for the high state of culture we are in, perhaps," answered John, who was leaning over his mother's chair, telling his day's experiences in a whisper.

"It is a merciful provision, my dears; for it takes three or four women to get each man into, through, and out of the world. You are costly creatures, boys; and it is well that mothers, sisters, wives, and daughters love their duty and do it so well, or you would perish off the face of the earth," said Mrs. Jo solemnly, as she took up a basket filled with dilapidated hose; for the good Professor was still hard on his socks, and his sons resembled him in that respect.

"Such being the case, there is a plenty for the 'superfluous women' to do, in taking care of these helpless men and their families. I see that more clearly every day, and am very glad and grateful that my profession will make me a useful, happy, and independent spinster."

Nan's emphasis on the last word caused Tom to groan, and the rest to laugh.

"I take great pride and solid satisfaction in you, Nan, and hope to see you very successful; for we do need just such helpful women in the world. I sometimes feel as if I'd missed my vocation and ought to have remained single; but my duty seemed to point this way, and I don't regret it," said Mrs. Jo, folding a large and very ragged blue sock to her bosom.

"Neither do I. What should I ever have done without my dearest Mum?" added Ted, with a filial hug which caused both to disappear behind the newspaper in which he had been mercifully absorbed for a few minutes.

"My darling boy, if you would wash your hands semi-occasionally, fond caresses would be less disastrous to my collar. Never mind, my precious tousle-head, better grass stains and dirt than no cuddlings at all." Mrs. Jo emerged from that brief eclipse looking much refreshed, though her back hair was caught in Ted's buttons and her collar under one ear.

Here Josie, who had been studying her part at the other end of the piazza, suddenly burst forth with a smothered shriek, and gave Juliet's speech in the tomb so effectively that the boys applauded, Daisy shivered, and Nan murmured, "Too much cerebral excitement for one of her age."

"I'm afraid you'll have to make up your mind to it, Meg. That child is a born actress. We never did anything so well, not even *The Witch's Curse*," said Mrs. Jo, casting a bouquet of many-colored socks at the feet of her flushed and panting niece, when she fell gracefully upon the door mat.

"It is a sort of judgment upon me for my passion for the stage when a girl. Now I know how dear Marmee felt when I begged to be an actress. I never can consent, and yet I may be obliged to give up my wishes, hopes, and plans again."

There was an accent of reproach in his mother's voice, which made Demi pick up his sister with a gentle shake, and the stern command to "drop that nonsense in public."

"Drop me, Minion, or I'll give you *The Maniac Bride*, with my best *ha-ha!*" cried Josie, glaring at him like an offended kitten.

Being set on her feet, she made a splendid curtsy and dramatically proclaiming "Mrs. Woffington's carriage waits," swept down the steps and round the corner, trailing Daisy's scarlet shawl majestically behind her.

"Isn't she great fun? I couldn't stop in this dull place if I hadn't that child to make it lively for me. If ever she turns prim, I'm off; so mind how you nip her in the bud," said Teddy, frowning at Demi, who was now writing out shorthand notes on the steps.

"You two are a team, and it takes a strong hand to drive you, but I rather like it. Josie ought to have been my child, and Rob yours, Meg. Then your house would have been all peace and mine all bedlam. Now I must go and tell Laurie the news. Come with me, Meg, a little stroll will do us good," and sticking Ted's straw hat on her head, Mrs. Jo walked off with her sister, leaving Daisy to attend to the muffins, Ted to appease Josie, and Tom and Nan to give their respective patients a very bad quarter of an hour.

2. Parnassus

IT WAS well named; and the Muses seemed to be at home
that day, for as the newcomers went up the slope appropriate sights and sounds greeted them. Passing an open window, they looked in upon a library presided over by Clio,
Calliope, and Urania; Melpomene and Thalia were disporting
themselves in the hall, where some young people were dancing
and rehearsing a play; Erato was walking in the garden with
her lover, and in the music room Phoebus himself was drilling
a tuneful choir.

A mature Apollo was our old friend Laurie, but comely
and genial as ever; for time had ripened the freakish boy into

a noble man. Care and sorrow, as well as ease and happiness, had done much for him; and the responsibility of carrying out his grandfather's wishes had been a duty most faithfully performed. Posperity suits some people, and they blossom best in a glow of sunshine; others need the shade, and are the sweeter for a touch of frost. Laurie was one of the former sort, and Amy was another; so life had been a kind of poem to them since they married—not only harmonious and happy, but earnest, useful, and rich in the beautiful benevolence which can do so much when wealth and wisdom go hand in hand with charity.

Their house was full of unostentatious beauty and comfort, and here the art-loving host and hostess attracted and entertained artists of all kinds. Laurie had music enough now, and was a generous patron to the class he most liked to help. Amy had her protégées among ambitious young painters and sculptors, and found her own art doubly dear as her daughter grew old enough to share its labors and delights with her; for she was one of those who prove that women can be faithful wives and mothers without sacrificing the special gift bestowed upon them for their own development and the good of others.

Her sisters knew where to find her, and Jo went at once to the studio, where mother and daughter worked together. Bess was busy with the bust of a little child, while her mother added the last touches to a fine head of her husband. Time seemed to have stood still with Amy, for happiness had kept her young and prosperity given her the culture she needed. A stately, graceful woman, who showed how elegant simplicity could be made by the taste with which she chose her dress and the grace with which she wore it. As someone said, "I never know what Mrs. Laurence has on, but I always receive the impression that she is the best-dressed lady in the room."

It was evident that she adored her daughter, and well she might; for the beauty she had longed for seemed, to her fond eyes at least, to be impersonated in this younger self. Bess inherited her mother's Dianalike figure, blue eyes, fair skin, and golden hair, tied up in the same classic knot of curls. Also—ah! never-ending source of joy to Amy—she had her father's handsome nose and mouth, cast in a feminine mold. The severe simplicity of a long linen pinafore suited her; and she worked away with the entire absorption of the true artist, unconscious of the loving eyes upon her, till Aunt Jo came in exclaiming eagerly:

"My dear girls, stop your mud pies and hear the news!"

Both artists dropped their tools and greeted the irrepressible woman cordially, though genius had been burning splendidly and her coming spoilt a precious hour. They were in the full tide of gossip when Laurie, who had been summoned by Meg, arrived, and sitting down between the sisters, with no barricade anywhere, listened with interest to the news of Franz and Emil.

"The epidemic has broken out, and now it will rage and ravage your flock. Be prepared for every sort of romance and rashness for the next ten years, Jo. Your boys are growing up and will plunge headlong into a sea of worse scrapes than any you have had yet," said Laurie, enjoying her look of mingled delight and despair.

"I know it, and I hope I shall be able to pull them through and land them safely; but it's an awful responsibility for they *will* come to me and insist that I can make their poor little loves run smoothly. I like it, though, and Meg is such a mush of sentiment she revels in the prospect," answered Jo, feeling pretty easy about her own boys, whose youth made them safe for the present.

"I'm afraid she won't revel when our Nat begins to buzz too near her Daisy. Of course you see what that all means? As musical director I am also his confidant, and would like to know what advice to give," said Laurie soberly.

"Hush! you forget that child," began Jo, nodding toward Bess, who was at work again.

"Bless you, she's in Athens, and doesn't hear a word. She ought to leave off, though, and go out. My darling, put the baby to sleep, and go for a run. Aunt Meg is in the parlor; go and show her the new pictures till we come," added Laurie, looking at his tall girl as Pygmalion might have looked at Galatea; for he considered her the finest statue in the house.

"Yes, papa; but please tell me if it is good." Bess obediently put down her tools, with a lingering glance at the bust.

"My cherished daughter, truth compels me to confess that one cheek is plumper than the other; and the curls upon its infant brow are rather too much like horns for perfect grace; otherwise it rivals Raphael's Chanting Cherubs, and I'm proud of it."

Laurie was laughing as he spoke; for these first attempts were so like Amy's early ones it was impossible to regard them as soberly as the enthusiastic mamma did.

"You can't see beauty in anything but music," answered Bess, shaking the golden head that made the one bright spot in the cool north lights of the great studio.

"Well, I see beauty in you, dear. And if you are not art, what is? I wish to put a little more nature into you, and get you away from this cold clay and marble into the sunshine, to dance and laugh as the others do. I want a flesh-and-blood girl, not a sweet statue in a gray pinafore, who forgets everything but her work."

As he spoke two dusty hands came round his neck, and Bess said earnestly, punctuating her words with soft touches of her lips:

"I never forget *you*, papa; but I do want to do something beautiful that you may be proud of me by and by. Mamma often tells me to stop; but when we get in here we forget there is any world outside, we are so busy and so happy. Now

I'll go and run and sing, and be a girl to please you." And throwing away the apron, Bess vanished from the room, seeming to take all the light with her.

"I'm glad you said that. The dear child *is* too much absorbed in her artistic dreams for one so young. It is my fault; but I sympathize so deeply in it all, I forget to be wise," sighed Amy, carefully covering the baby with a wet towel.

"I think this power of living in our children is one of the sweetest things in the world; but I try to remember what Marmee once said to Meg—that fathers should have their share in the education of both girls and boys; so I leave Ted to his father all I can, and Fritz lends me Rob, whose quiet ways are as restful and good for me as Ted's tempests are for his father. Now I advise you, Amy, to let Bess drop the mud pies for a time, and take up music with Laurie; then she won't be one-sided, and he won't be jealous."

"Hear, hear! A Daniel—a very Daniel!" cried Laurie, well pleased. "I thought you'd lend a hand, Jo, and say a word for me. I *am* a little jealous of Amy, and want more of a share in my girl. Come, my lady, let me have her this summer, and next year, when we go to Rome, I'll give her up to you and high art. Isn't that a fair bargain?"

"I agree; but in trying your hobby, nature, with music thrown in, don't forget that, though only fifteen, our Bess is older than most girls of that age, and cannot be treated like a child. She is so very precious to me, I feel as if I wanted to keep her always as pure and beautiful as the marble she loves so well."

Amy spoke regretfully as she looked about the lovely room where she had spent so many happy hours with this dear child of hers.

" 'Turn and turn about is fair play,' as we used to say when we all wanted to ride on Ellen Tree or wear the russet boots," said Jo briskly; "so you must share your girl between you, and see who will do the most for her."

"We will," answered the fond parents, laughing at the recollections Jo's proverb brought up to them.

"How I did use to enjoy bouncing on the limb of that old apple tree! No real horse ever gave me half the pleasure or the exercise," said Amy, looking out the high window as if she saw the dear old orchard again and the little girls at play there.

"And what fun I had with those blessed boots!" laughed Jo. "I've got the relics now. The boys reduced them to rags; but I love them still, and would enjoy a good theatrical stalk in them if it were possible."

"My fondest memories twine about the warming pan and the sausage. What larks we had! And how long ago it seems!" said Laurie, staring at the two women before him as if he found it hard to realize that they ever had been little Amy and riotous Jo.

"Don't suggest that we are growing old, my lord. We have only bloomed; and a very nice bouquet we make with our buds about us," answered Mrs. Amy, shaking out the folds of her rosy muslin with much the air of dainty satisfaction the girl used to show in a new dress.

"Not to mention our thorns and dead leaves," added Jo, with a sigh; for life had never been very easy to her, and even now she had her troubles both within and without.

"Come and have a dish of tea, old dear, and see what the young folks are about. You are tired, and want to be 'stayed with flagons and comforted with apples,'" said Laurie, offering an arm to each sister, and leading them away to afternoon tea, which flowed as freely on Parnassus as the nectar of old.

They found Meg in the summer parlor, an airy and delightful room, full now of afternoon sunshine and the rustle of trees; for the three long windows opened on the garden. The great music room was at one end, and at the other, in a deep alcove hung with purple curtains, a little household shrine had been made. Three portraits hung there, two marble busts stood in the corners, and a couch, an oval table, with its urn of flowers, were the only articles of furniture the nook contained. The busts were John Brooke and Beth—Amy's work —both excellent likenesses, and both full of the placid beauty which always recalls the saying that "Clay represents life; plaster, death; marble, immortality." On the right, as became the founder of the house, hung the portrait of Mr. Laurence, with its expression of mingled pride and benevolence, as fresh and attractive as when he caught the girl Jo admiring it. Opposite was Aunt March—a legacy to Amy—in an imposing turban, immense sleeves, and long mittens decorously crossed on the front of her plum-colored satin gown. Time had mellowed the severity of her aspect; and the fixed regard of the handsome old gentleman opposite seemed to account for the amiable simper on lips that had not uttered a sharp word for years.

In the place of honor, with the sunshine warm upon it, and a green garland always round it, was Marmee's beloved face, painted with grateful skill by a great artist whom she had befriended when poor and unknown. So beautifully lifelike was it that it seemed to smile down upon her daughters, saying cheerfully, "Be happy: I am with you still."

The three sisters stood a moment looking up at the beloved picture with eyes full of tender reverence and the longing that never left them; for this noble mother had been so much to them that no one could ever fill her place. Only two years since she had gone away to live and love anew, leaving such a sweet memory behind her that it was both an inspiration and a comforter to all the household. They felt this as they drew closer to one another, and Laurie put it into words as he said earnestly:

"I can ask nothing better for my child than that she may be a woman like our mother. Please God, she shall be, if I can do it; for I owe the best I have to this dear saint."

Just then a fresh voice began to sing "Ave Maria" in the music room, and Bess unconsciously echoed her father's prayer for her as she dutifully obeyed his wishes. The soft sound of the air Marmee used to sing led the listeners back into the world again from that momentary reaching after the loved and lost, and they sat down together near the open windows enjoying the music, while Laurie brought them tea, making the little service pleasant by the tender care he gave to it.

Nat came in with Demi, soon followed by Ted and Josie, the Professor and his faithful Rob, all anxious to hear more about "the boys." The rattle of cups and tongues grew brisk, and the setting sun saw a cheerful company resting in the bright room after the varied labors of the day.

Professor Bhaer was gray now, but robust and genial as ever; for he had the work he loved, and did it so heartily that the whole college felt his beautiful influence. Rob was as much like him as it was possible for a boy to be, and was already called the "young Professor," he so adored study and closely imitated his honored father in all ways.

"Well, heart's dearest, we go to have our boys again, all two, and many rejoice greatly," said Mr. Bhaer, seating himself beside Jo with a beaming face and a handshake of congratulation.

"Oh, Fritz, I'm so delighted about Emil, and if you approve about Franz also. Did you know Ludmilla? Is it a wise match?" asked Mrs. Jo, handing him her cup of tea and drawing closer, as if she welcomed her refuge in joy as well as sorrow.

"It all goes well. I saw the Mädchen when I went over to place Franz. A child then, but most sweet and charming. Blumenthal is satisfied, I think, and the boy will be happy.

He is too German to be content away from the Vaterland, so we shall have him as a link between the new and the old, and that pleases me much."

"And Emil, he is to be second mate next voyage, isn't that fine? I'm so happy that both *your* boys have done well; you gave up so much for them and their mother. You make light of it, dear, but I never forget it," said Jo, with her hand in his as sentimentally as if she was a girl again and her Fritz had come awooing.

He laughed his cheery laugh, and whispered behind her fan, "If I had not come to America for the poor lads, I never should have found my Jo. The hard times are very sweet now, and I bless Gott for all I seemed to lose, because I gained the blessing of my life."

"Spooning! Spooning! Here's an awful flirtation on the sly," cried Teddy, peering over the fan just at that interesting moment, much to his mother's confusion and his father's amusement; for the Professor never was ashamed of the fact that he still considered his wife the dearest woman in the world. Rob promptly ejected his brother from one window, to see him skip in at the other, while Mrs. Jo shut her fan and held it ready to rap her unruly boy's knuckles if he came near her again.

Nat approached in answer to Mr. Bhaer's beckoning tea-spoon, and stood before them with a face full of the respect-ful affection he felt for the excellent man who had done so much for him.

"I have the letters ready for thee, my son. They are to old friends of mine in Leipzig, who will befriend thee in that new life. It is well to have them for thou wilt be heartbroken with Heimweh at the first, Nat, and need comforting," said the Professor, giving him several letters.

"Thanks, sir. Yes, I expect to be pretty lonely till I get started, then my music and the hope of getting on will cheer me up," answered Nat, who both longed and dreaded to leave all these friends behind him and make new ones.

He was a man now; but the blue eyes were as honest as ever, the mouth still a little weak, in spite of the carefully cherished mustache over it, and the broad forehead more plainly than ever betrayed the music-loving nature of the youth. Modest, affectionate, and dutiful, Nat was considered a pleasant though not a brilliant success by Mrs. Jo. She loved and trusted him, and was sure he would do his best, but did not expect that he would be great in any way, unless the stimulus of foreign training and self-dependence made him a better artist and a stronger man than now seemed likely.

"I've marked all your things—or rather, Daisy did—and as soon as your books are collected, we can see about the packing," said Mrs. Jo, who was so used to fitting boys off for all quarters of the globe that a trip to the North Pole would not have been too much for her.

Nat grew red at mention of that name—or was it the last glow of sunset on his rather pale cheek?—and his heart beat happily at the thought of the dear girl working N's and B's on his humble socks and handkerchiefs; for Nat adored Daisy, and the cherished dream of his life was to earn a place for himself as a musician and win this angel for his wife. This hope did more for him than the Professor's counsels, Mrs. Jo's care, or Mr. Laurie's generous help. For her sake he worked, waited, and hoped, finding courage and patience in the dream of that happy future when Daisy should make a little home for him and he fiddle a fortune into her lap.

Mrs. Jo knew this; and though he was not exactly the man she would have chosen for her niece, she felt that Nat would always need just the wise and loving care Daisy could give him, and that without it there was danger of his being one of the amiable and aimless men who fail for want of the right pilot to steer them safely through the world. Mrs. Meg de-

cidedly frowned upon the poor boy's love and would not
hear of giving her dear girl to any but the best man to be
found on the face of the earth. She was very kind, but as firm
as such gentle souls can be; and Nat fled for comfort to Mrs.
Jo, who always espoused the interests of her boys heartily. A
new set of anxieties was beginning now that the aforesaid
boys were growing up, and she foresaw no end of worry as
well as amusement in the love affairs already budding in her
flock. Mrs. Meg was usually her best ally and adviser, for she
loved romances as well now as when a blooming girl herself.
But in this case she hardened her heart, and would not hear a
word of entreaty. "Nat was not man enough, never would be,
no one knew his family, a musician's life was a hard one; Daisy
was too young, five or six years hence when time had proved
both perhaps. Let us see what absence will do for him." And
that was the end of it, for when the maternal Pelican was
roused she could be very firm, though for her precious children she would have plucked her last feather and given the last
drop of her blood.

Mrs. Jo was thinking of this as she looked at Nat while he
talked with her husband about Leipzig, and she resolved to
have a clear understanding with him before he went; for she
was used to confidences, and talked freely with her boys about
the trials and temptations that beset all lives in the beginning,
and so often mar them, for want of the right word at the right
moment.

This is the first duty of parents, and no false delicacy should
keep them from the watchful care, the gentle warning, which
makes self-knowledge and self-control the compass and pilot
of the young as they leave the safe harbor of home.

"Plato and his disciples approach," announced irreverent
Teddy, as Mr. March came in with several young men and
women about him; for the wise old man was universally beloved, and ministered so beautifully to his flock that many of

them thanked him all their lives for the help given to both hearts and souls.

Bess went to him at once; for since Marmee died, grand-papa was her special care, and it was sweet to see the golden head bend over the silver one as she rolled out his easy chair and waited on him with tender alacrity.

"Aesthetic tea always on tap here, sir; will you have a flow-ing bowl or a bit of ambrosia?" asked Laurie, who was wan-dering about with a sugar basin in one hand and a plate of cake in the other; for sweetening cups and feeding the hun-gry was work he loved.

"Neither, thanks; this child has taken care of me." Mr. March turned to Bess, who sat on one arm of his chair, holding a glass of fresh milk.

"Long may she live to do it, sir, and I be here to see this pretty contradiction of the song that 'youth and age cannot live together!'" answered Laurie, smiling at the pair.

"'Crabbèd age,' papa; that makes all the difference in the world," said Bess quickly; for she loved poetry, and read the best.

> "Wouldst thou see fresh roses grow
> In a reverend bed of snow?"

quoted Mr. March, as Josie came and perched on the other arm, looking like a very thorny little rose; for she had been having a hot discussion with Ted, and had got the worst of it.

"Grandpa, must women always obey men and say they are the wisest, just because they are the strongest?" she cried, looking fiercely at her cousin, who came stalking up with a provoking smile on the boyish face that was always very comical atop of that tall figure.

"Well, my dear, that is the old-fashioned belief, and it will take some time to change it. But I think the woman's hour has struck; and it looks to me as if the boys must do their best, for the girls are abreast now, and may reach the goal first," answered Mr. March, surveying with paternal satisfaction the bright faces of the young women, who were among the best students in the college.

"The poor little Atalantas are sadly distracted and delayed by the obstacles thrown in their way—not golden apples, by any means—but I think they will stand a fair chance when they have learned to run better," laughed Uncle Laurie, stroking Josie's breezy hair, which stood up like the fur of an angry kitten.

"Whole barrels of apples won't stop me when *I* start, and a dozen Teds won't trip me up, though they may try. I'll show him that a woman can act as well, if not better, than a man. It *has* been done, and will be again; and I'll never own that *my* brain isn't as good as his, though it may be smaller," cried the excited young person.

"If you shake your head in that violent way, you'll addle what brains you have got; and I'd take care of 'em, if I were you," began teasing Ted.

"What started this civil war?" asked grandpapa, with a gentle emphasis on the adjective, which caused the combatants to calm their ardor a little.

"Why, we were pegging away at the *Iliad* and came to where Zeus tells Juno not to inquire into his plans or he'll whip her, and Jo was disgusted because Juno meekly hushed up. I said it was all right, and agreed with the old fellow that women didn't know much and ought to obey men," explained Ted, to the great amusement of his hearers.

"Goddesses may do as they like, but those Greek and Trojan women were poor-spirited things if they minded men who couldn't fight their own battles and had to be hustled off by Pallas, and Venus, and Juno, when they were going to get beaten. The idea of two armies stopping and sitting down

while a pair of heroes flung stones at one another! I don't
think much of your old Homer. Give me Napoleon or Grant
for my hero."

Josie's scorn was as funny as if a hummingbird scolded at
an ostrich, and everyone laughed as she sniffed at the immor-
tal poet and criticized the gods.

"Napoleon's Juno had a nice time; didn't she? That's just
the way girls argue—first one way and then the other," jeered
Ted.

"Like Johnson's young lady, who was 'not categorical, but
all wiggle-waggle,'" added Uncle Laurie, enjoying the battle
immensely.

"I was only speaking of them as soldiers. But if you come to
the woman side of it, wasn't Grant a kind husband and Mrs.
Grant a happy woman? He didn't threaten to whip her if she
asked a natural question; and if Napoleon did do wrong about
Josephine, he could fight, and didn't want any Minerva to
come fussing over him. They *were* a stupid set, from dandified
Paris to Achilles sulking in his ships, and I won't change my
opinion for all the Hectors and Agamemnons in Greece," said
Josie, still unconquered.

"You can fight like a Trojan, that's evident; and we will
be the two obedient armies looking on while you and Ted have
it out," began Uncle Laurie, assuming the attitude of a warrior
leaning on his spear.

"I fear we must give it up, for Pallas is about to descend
and carry off our Hector," said Mr. March, smiling, as Jo
came to remind her son that suppertime was near.

"We will fight it out later when there are no goddesses to
interfere," said Teddy, as he turned away with unusual
alacrity, remembering the treat in store.

"Conquered by a muffin, by Jove!" called Josie after him,
exulting in an opportunity to use the classical exclamation
forbidden to her sex.

But Ted shot a Parthian arrow as he retired in good order by replying, with a highly virtuous expression, "Obedience is a soldier's first duty."

Bent on her woman's privilege of having the last word, Josie ran after him, but never uttered the scathing speech upon her lips, for a very brown young man in a blue suit came leaping up the steps with a cheery "Ahoy! Ahoy! where is everybody?"

"Emil! Emil!" cried Josie, and in a moment Ted was upon him, and the late enemies ended their fray in a joyful welcome to the newcomer.

Muffins were forgotten; and towing their cousin like two fussy little tugs with a fine merchantman, the children returned to the parlor, where Emil kissed all the women and shook hands with all men except his uncle; him he embraced in the good old German style, to the great delight of the observers.

"Didn't think I could get off today, but found I could, and steered straight for old Plum. Not a soul there, so I luffed and bore away for Parnassus, and here is every man jack of you. Bless your hearts, how glad I am to see you all!" exclaimed the sailor boy, beaming at them, as he stood with his legs apart as if he still felt the rocking deck under his feet.

"You ought to 'shiver your timbers,' not 'bless our hearts,' Emil; it's not nautical at all. Oh, how nice and shippy and tarry you do smell!" said Josie, sniffing at him with great enjoyment of the fresh sea odors he brought with him. This was her favorite cousin, and she was his pet; so she knew that the bulging pockets of the blue jacket contained treasures for her at least.

"Avast, my hearty, and let me take soundings before you dive," laughed Emil, understanding her affectionate caresses, and holding her off with one hand while with the other he rummaged out sundry foreign little boxes and parcels marked with different names, and handed them round with appropriate remarks, which caused much laughter; for Emil was a wag.

"There's a hawser that will hold our little cockboat still about five minutes," he said, throwing a necklace of pretty pink coral over Josie's head; "and here's something the mermaids sent to Undine," he added, handing Bess a string of pearly shells on a silver chain. "I thought Daisy would like a fiddle, and Nat can find her a *beau*," continued the sailor, with a laugh, as he undid a dainty filigree brooch in the shape of a violin.

"I know she will, and I'll take it to her," answered Nat, as he vanished, glad of an errand, and sure that *he* could find Daisy though Emil had missed her.

Emil chuckled, and handed out a quaintly carved bear whose head opened, showing a capacious inkstand. This he presented, with a scrape, to Aunt Jo.

"Knowing your fondness for these fine animals, I brought this one to your pen."

"Very good, Commodore! Try again," said Mrs. Jo, much pleased with her gift, which caused the Professor to prophesy "works of Shakespeare" from its depths, so great would be the inspiration of the beloved bruin.

"As Aunt Meg *will* wear caps, in spite of her youth, I got Ludmilla to get me some bits of lace. Hope you'll like 'em," and out of a soft paper came some filmy things, one of which soon lay like a net of snowflakes on Mrs. Meg's pretty hair.

"I couldn't find anything swell enough for Aunt Amy, because she has everything she wants, so I brought a little picture that always makes me think of her when Bess was a baby," and he handed her an oval ivory locket, on which was painted a golden-haired Madonna with a rosy child folded in her blue mantle.

"How lovely!" cried everyone; and Aunt Amy at once hung it about her neck on the blue ribbon from Bess's hair, charmed with her gift; for it recalled the happiest year of her life.

"Now, I flatter myself I've got just the thing for Nan, neat but not gaudy, a sort of sign you see, and very appropriate for a doctor," said Emil, proudly displaying a pair of lava ear-rings shaped like little skulls.

"Horrid!" Bess, who hated ugly things, turned her eyes to her own pretty shells.

"She won't wear earrings," said Josie.

"Well, she'll enjoy punching your ears then. She's never so happy as when she's overhauling her fellow creatures and going for 'em with a knife," answered Emil, undisturbed. "I've got a lot of plunder for you fellows in my chest, but I knew I should have no peace till my cargo for the girls was un-loaded. Now tell me all the news." And, seated on Amy's best marble-topped table, the sailor swung his legs and talked at the rate of ten knots an hour, till Aunt Jo carried them all off to a grand family tea in honor of the Commodore.

3. Jo's Last Scrape

THE March family had enjoyed a great many surprises in the course of their varied career, but the greatest of all was when the Ugly Duckling turned out to be, not a swan, but a golden goose, whose literary eggs found such an unexpected market that in ten years Jo's wildest and most cherished dream actually came true. How or why it happened she never clearly understood, but all of a sudden she found herself famous in a small way, and, better still, with a snug little fortune in her pocket to clear away the obstacles of the present and assure the future of her boys.

It began during a bad year when everything went wrong

at Plumfield: times were hard, the school dwindled, Jo over-worked herself and had a long illness; Laurie and Amy were abroad, and the Bhaers too proud to ask help even of those as near and dear as this generous pair. Confined to her room, Jo got desperate over the state of affairs, till she fell back upon the long-disused pen as the only thing she could do to help fill up the gaps in the income. A book for girls being wanted by a certain publisher, she hastily scribbled a little story describing a few scenes and adventures in the lives of herself and sisters—though boys were more in her line—and with very slight hopes of success sent it out to seek its fortune.

Things always went by contraries with Jo. Her first book, labored over for years, and launched full of the high hopes and ambitious dreams of youth, foundered on its voyage, though the wreck continued to float long afterward, to the profit of the publisher at least. The hastily written story, sent away with no thought beyond the few dollars it might bring, sailed with a fair wind and a wise pilot at the helm straight into public favor, and came home heavily laden with an un-expected cargo of gold and glory.

A more astonished woman probably never existed than Josephine Bhaer when her little ship came into port with flags flying, cannon that had been silent before now booming gaily, and, better than all, many kind faces rejoicing with her, many friendly hands grasping hers with cordial congratulations. After that it was plain sailing, and she merely had to load her ships and send them off on prosperous trips, to bring home stores of comfort for all she loved and labored for.

The fame she never did quite accept; for it takes very little fire to make a great deal of smoke nowadays, and notoriety is not real glory. The fortune she could not doubt, and grate-fully received; though it was not half so large a one as a generous world reported it to be. The tide, having turned, con-tinued to rise and floated the family comfortably into a snug harbor where the older members could rest secure from storms, and whence the younger ones could launch their boats for the voyage of life.

All manner of happiness, peace, and plenty came in those years to bless the patient waiters, hopeful workers, and devout believers in the wisdom and justice of Him who sends disappointment, poverty, and sorrow to try the love of human hearts and make success the sweeter when it comes. The world saw the prosperity, and kind souls rejoiced over the improved fortunes of the family; but the success Jo valued most, the happiness that nothing could change or take away, few knew much about.

It was the power of making her mother's last years happy and serene; to see the burden of care laid down forever, the weary hands at rest, the dear face untroubled by any anxiety, and the tender heart free to pour itself out in the wise charity which was its delight. As a girl, Jo's favorite plan had been a room where Marmee could sit in peace and enjoy herself after her hard, heroic life. Now the dream had become a happy fact, and Marmee sat in her pleasant chamber with every comfort and luxury about her, loving daughters to wait on her as infirmities increased, a faithful mate to lean upon, and grandchildren to brighten the twilight of life with their dutiful affection. A very precious time to all, for she rejoiced as only mothers can in the good fortunes of their children. She had lived to reap the harvest she sowed; had seen prayers answered, hopes blossom, good gifts bear fruit, peace and prosperity bless the home she had made; and then, like some brave, patient angel, whose work was done, turned her face heavenward, glad to rest.

This was the sweet and sacred side of the change; but it had its droll and thorny one, as all things have in this curious world of ours. After the first surprise, incredulity, and joy which came to Jo, with the ingratitude of human nature, she soon tired of renown and began to resent her loss of liberty. For suddenly the admiring public took possession of her and all her affairs, past, present, and to come. Strangers demanded to look at her, question, advise, warn, congratulate, and drive her out of her wits by well-meant but very wearisome attentions. If she declined to open her heart to them, they reproached her; if she refused to endow pet charities, relieve private wants, or sympathize with every ill and trial known to humanity, she was called hardhearted, selfish, and haughty; if she found it impossible to answer the piles of letters sent her, she was neglectful of her duty to the admiring public; and if she preferred the privacy of home to the pedestal upon which she was requested to pose, "the airs of literary people" were freely criticized.

She did her best for the children, they being the public for whom she wrote, and labored stoutly to supply the demand always in the mouths of voracious youth—"More stories; more right away!" Her family objected to this devotion at their expense, and her health suffered; but for a time she gratefully offered herself up on the altar of juvenile literature, feeling that she owed a good deal to the little friends in whose sight she had found favor after twenty years of effort.

But a time came when her patience gave out and, wearying of being a lion, she became a bear in nature as in name, and retiring to her den, growled awfully when ordered out. Her family enjoyed the fun, and had small sympathy with her trials, but Jo came to consider it the worst scrape of her life; for liberty had always been her dearest possession, and it seemed to be fast going from her. Living in a lantern soon loses its charms, and she was too old, too tired, and too busy to like it. She felt that she had done all that could reasonably be required of her when autographs, photographs, and autobiographical sketches had been sown broadcast over the land; when artists had taken her home in all its aspects, and report-

ers had taken her in the grim one she always assumed on these
trying occasions; when a series of enthusiastic boarding schools
had ravaged her grounds for trophies, and a steady stream of
amiable pilgrims had worn her doorsteps with their respectful
feet; when servants left after a week's trial of the bell that
rang all day; when her husband was forced to guard her at
meals, and the boys to cover her retreat out of back windows
on certain occasions when enterprising guests walked in un-
announced at unfortunate moments.

A sketch of one day may perhaps explain the state of things,
offer some excuse for the unhappy woman, and give a hint to
the autograph fiend now rampant in the land; for it is a true
tale.

"There ought to be a law to protect unfortunate authors,"
said Mrs. Jo one morning soon after Emil's arrival, when the
mail brought her an unusually large and varied assortment of
letters. "To me it is a more vital subject than international
copyright; for time is money, peace is health, and I lose both
with no return but less respect for my fellow creatures and a
wild desire to fly into the wilderness, since I cannot shut my
doors even in free America."

"Lion hunters are awful when in search of their prey. If
they could change places for a while it would do them good;
and they'd see what bores they were when they 'do themselves the honor of calling to express their admiration of our
charming work,' " quoted Ted, with a bow to his parent, now
frowning over twelve requests for autographs.

"I have made up my mind on one point," said Mrs. Jo with
great firmness. "I will *not* answer this kind of letter. I've sent
at least six to this boy, and he probably sells them. This girl
writes from a seminary, and if I send her one all the other girls
will at once write for more. All begin by saying they know
they intrude, and that I am of course annoyed by these requests; but they venture to ask because I like boys, or they

like the books, or it is only one. Emerson and Whittier put
these things in the wastepaper basket; and though only a literary nursery maid who provides moral pap for the young, I
will follow their illustrious example; for I shall have no time
to eat or sleep if I try to satisfy these dear unreasonable children." And Mrs. Jo swept away the entire batch with a sigh
of relief.

"I'll open the others and let you eat your breakfast in peace,
liebe Mutter," said Rob, who often acted as her secretary.
"Here's one from the South," and breaking an imposing seal,
he read:

> MADAM, As it has pleased Heaven to bless your efforts with
> a large fortune, I feel no hesitation in asking you to supply
> funds to purchase a new communion service for our church.
> To whatever denomination you belong, you will of course
> respond with liberality to such a request.
> Respectfully yours,   MRS. X. Y. ZAVIER

"Send a civil refusal, dear. All I have to give must go to
feed and clothe the poor at my gates. That is my thank offering for success. Go on," answered his mother, with a grateful
glance about her happy home.

"A literary youth of eighteen proposes that you put your
name to a novel he has written; and after the first edition your
name is to be taken off and his put on. There's a cool proposal
for you. I guess you won't agree to that, in spite of your soft-
heartedness toward most of the young scribblers."

"Couldn't be done. Tell him so kindly, and don't let him
send the manuscript. I have seven on hand now, and barely
time to read my own," said Mrs. Jo, pensively fishing a small
letter out of the slop bowl and opening it with care, because
the downhill address suggested that a child wrote it.

"I will answer this myself. A little sick girl wants a book, and she shall have it, but I can't write sequels to all the rest to please her. I should never come to an end if I tried to suit these voracious little Oliver Twists, clamoring for more. What next, Robin?"

"This is short and sweet."

> DEAR MRS. BHAER, I am now going to give you my opinion of your works. I have read them all many times, and call them first-rate. Please go ahead.
>
> Your admirer, BILLY BABCOCK

"Now that is what I like. Billy is a man of sense and a critic worth having, since he has read my works many times before expressing his opinion. He asks for no answer, so send my thanks and regards."

"Here's a lady in England with seven girls, and she wishes to know your views upon education. Also what careers they shall follow—the oldest being twelve. Don't wonder she's worried," laughed Rob.

"I'll try to answer it. But as I have no girls, my opinion isn't worth much and will probably shock her, as I shall tell her to let them run and play and build up good, stout bodies before she talks about careers. They will soon show what they want, if they are let alone and not all run in the same mold."

"Here's a fellow who wants to know what sort of a girl he shall marry, and if you know of any like those in your stories."

"Give him Nan's address, and see what he'll get," proposed Ted, privately resolving to do it himself if possible.

"This is from a lady who wants you to adopt her child and lend her money to study art abroad for a few years. Better take it, and try your hand at a girl, mother."

"No, thank you, I will keep to my own line of business. What is that blotted one? It looks rather awful, to judge by

the ink," asked Mrs. Jo, who beguiled her daily task by trying
to guess from the outside what was inside her many letters.
This proved to be a poem from an insane admirer, to judge by
its incoherent style.

To J. M. B.

Oh, were I a heliotrope,
   I would play poet,
And blow a breeze of fragrance
   To you; and none should know it.

Your form like the stately elm
   When Phœbus gilds the morning ray;
Your cheeks like the ocean bed
   That blooms a rose in May.

Your words are wise and bright,
   I bequeath them to you a legacy given;
And when your spirit takes its flight,
   May it bloom a flower in heaven.

My tongue in flattering language spoke,
And sweeter silence never broke
In busiest street or loneliest glen.
I take you with the flashes of my pen.

Consider the lilies, how they grow;
   They toil not, yet are fair,
Gems and flowers and Solomon's seal.
   The geranium of the world is J. M. Bhaer.

                       JAMES

   While the boys shouted over this effusion—which is a true
one—their mother read several liberal offers from budding
magazines for her to edit them gratis; one long letter from a

young girl inconsolable because her favorite hero died, and "would dear Mrs. Bhaer rewrite the tale, and make it end good?"; another from an irate boy denied an autograph, who darkly foretold financial ruin and loss of favor if she did not send him and all other fellows who asked autographs, photographs, and autobiographical sketches; a minister wished to know her religion; and an undecided maiden asked which of her two lovers she should marry. These samples will suffice to show a few of the claims made on a busy woman's time and make my readers pardon Mrs. Jo if she did not carefully reply to all.

"That job is done. Now I will dust a bit, and then go to my work. I'm all behindhand, and serials can't wait; so deny me to everybody, Mary. I won't see Queen Victoria if she comes today." And Mrs. Bhaer threw down her napkin as if defying all creation.

"I hope the day will go well with thee, my dearest," answered her husband, who had been busy with his own voluminous correspondence. "I will dine at college with Professor Plock, who is to visit us today. The Jünglings can lunch on Parnassus; so thou shalt have a quiet time." And smoothing the worried lines out of her forehead with his good-by kiss, the excellent man marched away, both pockets full of books, an old umbrella in one hand and a bag of stones for the geology class in the other.

"If all literary women had such thoughtful angels for husbands, they would live longer and write more. Perhaps that wouldn't be a blessing to the world though, as most of us write too much now," said Mrs. Jo waving her feather duster to her spouse, who responded with flourishes of the umbrella as he went down the avenue.

Rob started for school at the same time, looking so much like him with his books and bag and square shoulders and steady air that his mother laughed as she turned away, saying